Outrageous Fashion

Dear Reader

When I asked boys and girls of your age if they wanted me to write a book about fashion, they all said, "YES!"

> THE FASHION DESIGN PROCESS ALWAYS STARTS WITH IDEAS AND FINISHES WITH PRODUCTS!

Then I asked which title they liked: *Fashion is Fun* or *Outrageous Fashion*? The students said both, so I chose the title that sounded the coolest!

I hope you enjoy reading about some of the people creating outrageous and practical fashion – from surf wear to circus handbags, to life jackets for dogs.

Sharon Parsons

My sincere thanks to the following people for their time, information, images and enthusiasm for this book:

Sam Brown, Munster Clothes, Sydney, Australia
Lulu Guinness, London, United Kingdom
Sophie Cobold, London, United Kingdom
Jodie Kiddle, Rip Curl, Torquay, Australia
Ruff Wear Inc, Oregon, USA

Contents

OUTRAGEOUS Fashion

Design "in Fashion" Products

What do we mean when we say that something is "in fashion"? Usually it means that people think a new product looks so good, they want to buy it and wear it.

Let's say the product is a new style of jeans for kids. The jeans will be in fashion when most kids love the design and want to buy and wear them. A fashion design process for jeans is on page 6.

Fashion for Seasons

Clothing fashions can change from season to season and year to year. Colours and types of fabrics can also change. For example, if jeans were designed for summer, they may be made with a light cotton fabric.

Fabric for Fashion

Designers need to know about all kinds of fabrics. Natural fabrics include wool, silk, cotton and linen. Synthetic fabrics include polyester, nylon, viscose and rayon.

a fabric swatch

Fashion **Design** Process

The fashion design process always starts with ideas and finishes with products!

Aim: Design Jeans for 2020

Imagine you need to design and make a new pair of jeans for kids in the year 2020. This is how you might design them in ten steps.

A mood board example

1 Think of Ideas

Create a "mood board" to help you imagine the style and colour of the jeans. Use pictures and fabric samples.

2 Draw Your Ideas

Draw lots of designs for your new jeans based on the "mood board" style and colour.

3 Final Design

Draw the final design to show all the details such as pockets, zips and buttons.

4 Create a Pattern

Use the final design to create a paper pattern for your jeans. Make the paper pattern by drawing an outline of each of the pieces. Cut out the pattern.

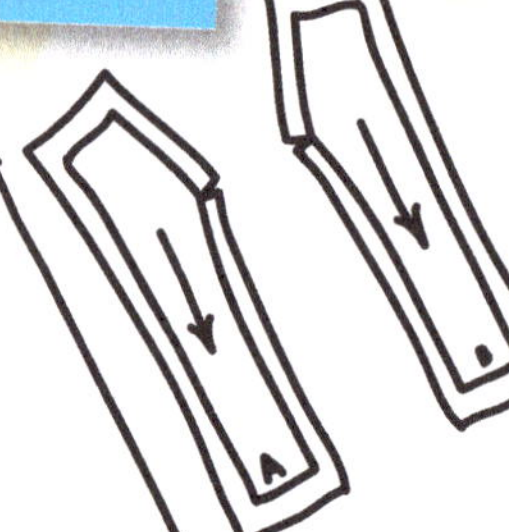

5 Choose Fabric

Next, decide which is the best fabric to use. Denim is a good choice for jeans.

Denim Fabric

Denim was once used for workers' trousers because it was hard-wearing. It became a popular fabric for clothes in the 1950s. At that time, some schools in the USA banned students from wearing denim.

a denim fabric swatch

6 Lay Out

Lay out the fabric. Place the pattern pieces on the fabric. Then pin them on so that they don't move.

7 Cut Out Pieces

Then carefully cut the fabric around each of the pattern pieces. The fabric pieces are now ready to sew together.

8 Sew Jeans

Now it's time to start stitching. Sew the fabric pieces together to make your new pair of jeans.

9 Final Details

Add the final details, such as zips and buttons.

10 Try on Jeans!

Do the jeans fit? YES!

2 Fashion for Boys

Munster or **"Monster"** Clothes?

Sam is a fashion designer for kids' clothes. She started by designing clothes for her three sons. First Sam created a scary, misbehaving character called Mikey Munster. Mikey Munster had a fat, pudgy nose and white pointy teeth. Then she thought about what sort of clothes her character would like to wear. She knew that her three sons would like to wear clothes just like the ones that Mikey wore.

Munster Kids Clothes

When people saw Sam's boys wearing Mikey Munster clothes, they liked them so Sam started to design clothes for all boys. Today, Sam and her team design clothes for boys, girls and toddlers.

Munster Clothes Names

Sam and her team created cool names for each piece of clothing. For the winter tops, they created names like Jaws, People Eater and Smashem.

DO YOU WANT SHARK'S TEETH ON YOUR JAWS JACKET?

Pillow-Fight Fashion

Sam's sons loved pillow-fights so she designed some pillows. Kids love to sleep on them and play with them!

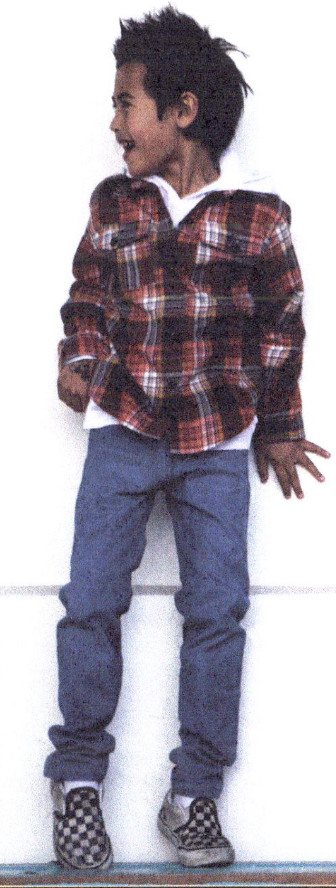

Fashion Design Tip
Fashion designers should always listen to their customers and design clothes that they want to buy.

Outrageous Accessories

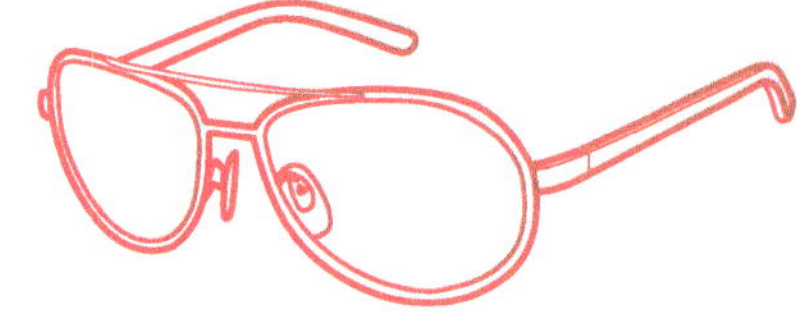

From **Hats** Down to **Shoes**

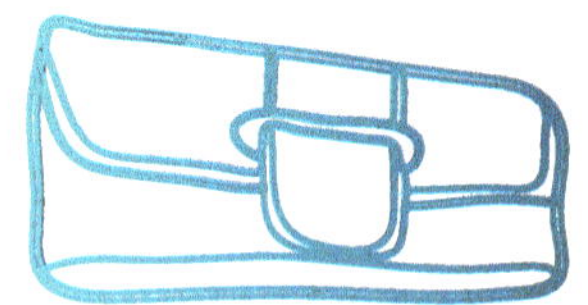

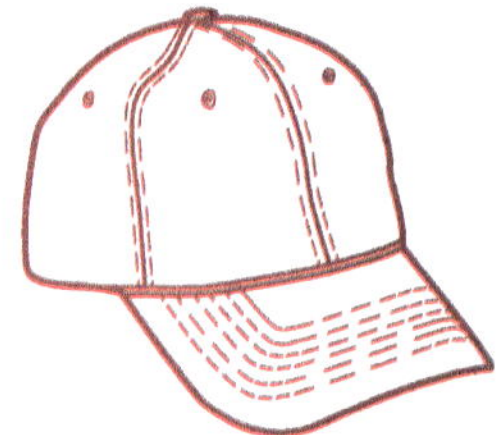

Not all accessories have to be outrageous. But they should be useful. Accessories are things like hats, bags, shoes, scarves, gloves, belts, sunglasses and jewellery.

Fashion for accessories can change from year to year. But if you choose accessories carefully, you can use them for many years!

Questions to Ask

When you buy accessories, ask yourself questions such as:

- Does this hat fit my head? Will it keep the sun off my face, neck and ears?
- Will this bag carry all the things I need?
- Do these shoes fit my feet?
- Will this scarf keep me warm?
- Will these sunglasses protect my eyes?
- Will this belt hold up my jeans?
- Will this bracelet stay on my wrist?

An Outrageous Bag Story

One day I was on a shopping mission – to find an outrageous bag. As I looked around the shop, all I could see were ordinary black, brown and white bags. And suddenly … there it was!

AN OUTRAGEOUS

BAG!

I loved the circus bag so much I searched the Internet to find out who designed it.

The person who designed the bag was Lulu Guinness – a successful fashion designer who lives in London, England.

THAT DAY I BECAME A FAN OF LULU'S BAGS!

If you're interested in outrageous fashion accessories, you'll love Lulu's story in Chapter Four!

Outrageous and GLAMorous!

Fashion Designer, Lulu Guinness

One hot, summer night in December, I phoned Lulu Guinness for an interview. For Lulu, it was a chilly winter's morning.

Not only was Lulu in a different season, it was also a different time in London! I was excited to ask Lulu questions about why she uses animals and pictures of big, red lips on her products.

Author's Place
Melbourne, Australia
Season: Summer
Time: 7.10 pm

Lulu's Place
London, England
Season: Winter
Time: 10.10 am

Lulu takes her daughters and a friend out for a special night.

Let's Interview Lulu

After I thanked Lulu for her time, I asked her questions about being a fashion designer.

 Q: Why are animal images used on many of your bags?

 A: I love animals and they're so much fun.

 Q: Why are red lips on many of your bags?

 A: I love red and I always wear red lipstick.

 Q: Are the red lip designs used on other accessories too?

 A: Yes, it's part of my brand. When people see red lips in my designs, they say, "That's a Lulu Guinness bag!"

 Q: Why is a brand important?

 A: It's important in fashion to have a brand that stands out so people will recognise my products immediately.

 Q: Why are your designs so much fun?

 A: I love to create fun designs so people smile and enjoy my products.

See some of Lulu's fantastic accessories on pages 14–15

What's your favourite bag?
Kooky cat collection
Chocolate bag
Bird cage
SILVER SHELL
Fish purse

Shop front

Poodle parlour

Poodle pamper

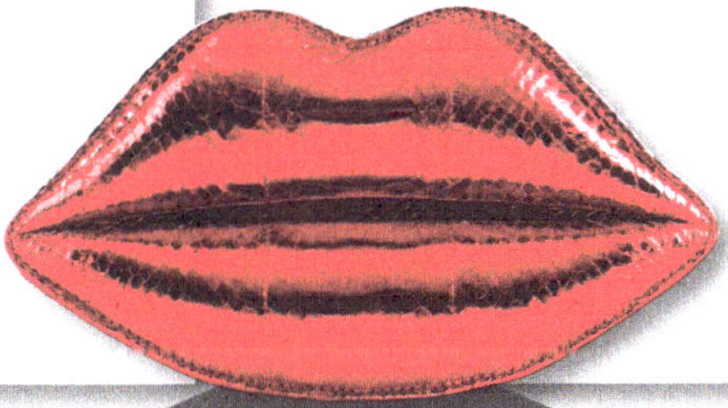

RED LIPS

Birdcage bags

First Twenty Years in Fashion

This history timeline shows how Lulu became a famous fashion designer.

From One Bag to Many Accessories!

Kooky cat jewellery

1989	Lulu designs her first bag.
1990	Lulu designs more handbags.
1996	Lulu opens her first store in London, England. Celebrities like Madonna bought her handbags!
1998	Lulu opens another store in London.
2000	Lulu opens a store in New York, USA.
2002	Lulu starts designing accessories such as shoes, socks and umbrellas.
2003	Lulu starts designing other accessories such as scarves and sunglasses. Lulu opens a new store in Japan.
2004	Lulu starts designing stationery, such as notepads and envelopes.
2005	Lulu designs a range of glasses for the USA.
2006	Lulu starts designing jewellery.
2008	Lulu designs more accessories. Lulu loves poodles. Look at her poodle bags!
2009	Lulu celebrates her 20th anniversary with a party at London's Victoria and Albert Museum.

a Lulu umbrella

a poodle pamper bag

Today, Lulu continues to design!

Arts and Economics

Fashion Ideas

Fashion designers can have hundreds of ideas, but they usually start by designing one product or a small collection. If that is successful, they will probably design more products.

Do You Want to Be a Fashion Designer?

If you want to be a fashion designer, Lulu says:

"USE YOUR IMAGINATION AND DESIGN THINGS THAT YOU LOVE. HAVE CONFIDENCE IN YOURSELF, AND DARE TO BE DIFFERENT!"

Lulu Designs a Bag for a Hospital

Lulu designed a bag for the world's first cancer hospital in London – The Royal Marsden.

the Royal Marsden bag

The money raised from sales of the bag is used for cancer research and some special hospital projects.

Social Studies

Lulu's Royal Award

In 2006, Lulu was presented with an award from the Queen of England for her great work in the arts.

Thank you Lulu for showing us that fashion can be fun and outrageous!

5 Fashion Shows

People **Work** Together

A fashion show is an exciting event where fashion designers show their latest fashions. Many people work together to make a fashion show exciting and colourful:

- models
- fashion designers
- fashion buyers
- fashion magazine reviewers
- make-up and hair stylists
- catwalk designers and builders
- lighting crew
- musicians
- fashion photographers.

walking the catwalk

CATWALKS

The narrow ramps that models walk along in fashion shows are called catwalks or runways.

Fashion is all about trends!

Barbie's 50th Birthday

The first Barbie doll was created in 1959.

In 2009, Barbie turned 50 years old. Around the world there were many fashionable events to celebrate this famous doll's birthday.

Ruth Handler created Barbie in America in 1959. Ruth got the idea from her daughter Barbara. Barbara and her friends used dolls to tell stories of the future. Ruth named the doll Barbie after her daughter.

Fashion Event Companies

Fashion shows need to be planned carefully.

Fashion event companies can do all the organising. They plan and organise:

- the hair and make-up artists
- the models
- the venue
- the theme
- the food
- the music.

getting ready

hair and make-up

on the catwalk

6 Surf Fashion

A **Surf-Wear** Designer

Imagine this … Jodie loves surfing, she works near a surf beach and her job is to design surf clothing!

Jodie designs swimwear and board shorts for teenage girls. She loves her job.

AWESOME!

Maths and Technology

Maths for Designers

Clothes designers need to be good at maths and technology, too. Designers must work out measurements for designs to suit different-shaped bodies. To work out patterns, designers must understand sizes, shapes and angles.

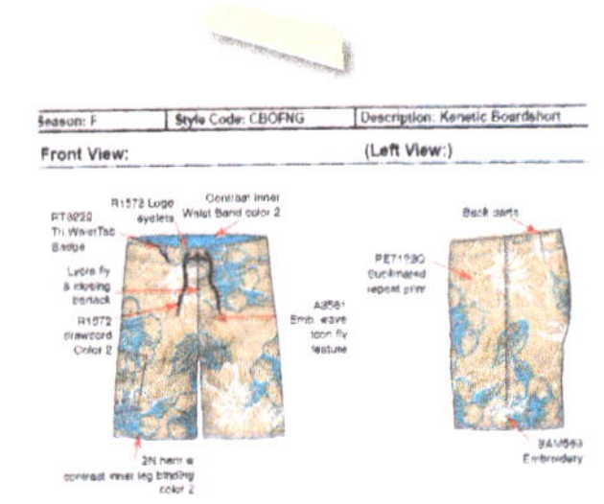

a template for board shorts

Designers must also understand fabric technology to work out the best fabric for each design.

Jodie's Design Year

Design 1st summer range	May, June, July, August
Design 2nd summer range	September, October, November, December
Design winter range	January, February, March
Travel to research fashion	April

In April, Jodie goes to Europe and the USA to research fashion styles.

Jodie's Deadlines

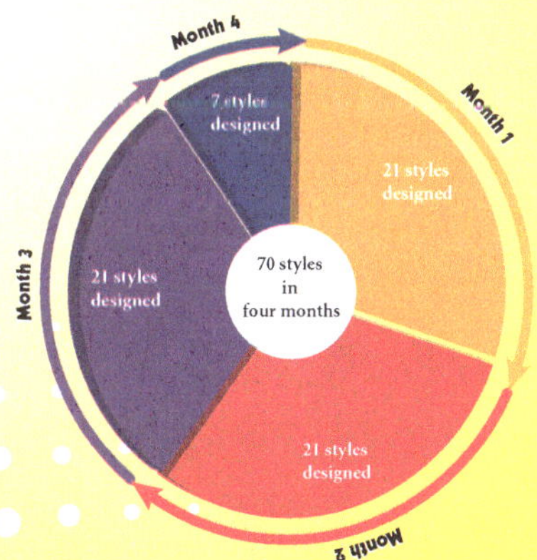

Jodie usually designs 70 new styles of swimwear and board shorts for the first summer range – in four months.

Fashion Forecasting

When a fashion designer predicts what people might wear in the future, it is called fashion forecasting. Jodie travels to cities in the Northern Hemisphere to see which fashions are most popular. It helps her to fashion forecast surf wear for teenagers.

Jodie at work

JODIE DESIGNED 70 NEW STYLES IN FOUR MONTHS!

Advice for Design Students

Jodie says that there are many jobs if you are interested in drawing and fashion design. It's helpful if you get good marks in: arts, graphic design, english, maths and technology.

You need to work hard and really love designing!

> "I LOVE MY JOB. I GET TO CREATE AND DRAW EVERY DAY."
> JODIE

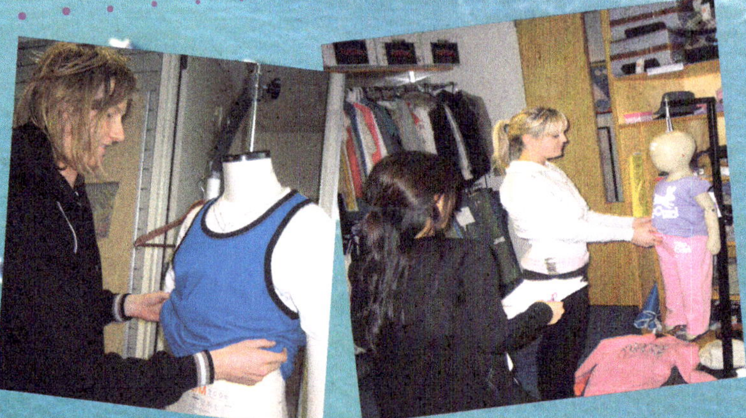

Surf-wear designers put their new designs on models to see how they look and fit.

board shorts modelled by surfers

7 Fashionable DOGS!

Practical **Fashion** for Dogs

Dog owners can buy clothes and accessories for their pooches, such as coats, collars, shoes, name tags, and even life jackets for swimming.

Designers create colourful and appealing accessories that are practical for the dogs but also fun!

Dog Coats

In the winter, many dogs wear dog coats to keep dry and warm. Dog coats are important for puppies, little dogs, sick dogs and older dogs.

Dogs can wear OUTRAGEOUS fashion, too!

Index

Glossary

cancer hospital	A hospital specialising in the treatment of patients who are ill with cancer
fabric technology	The way people apply their knowledge of fabrics, and how they behave, to make better clothes
graphic design	The way people put together colours, designs and ideas on paper
mood board	A collection of colours, fabrics and patterns that a designer uses to create a theme for a product
Northern Hemisphere	The northern half of a sphere, in this case Earth, lying above the equator
rayon	A fabric made from sticky plant materials that have been crushed and made into threads
synthetic fabrics	Artificial fabrics that have been made by chemical processes, rather than grown naturally
viscose	A thick liquid made from plant pulp and used to manufacture rayon and cellophane